SCIENCE COURT

TO SERVE AND OBSERVE™

The Case of the Dear Departed Chicken Bone

Adapted by Craig Strasshofer

Based on an orginal TV episode written and created by Tom Snyder, Bill Braudis, and David Dockterman

Illustrated by Bob Thibeault and Kristine Koob

Troll

BETTER READ THAN DEAD

Alison Krempel and her assistant Tim were strolling through the park one fine day. They were talking about two of their favorite things, science and the law. Alison was a Science Court attorney—dedicated, hard-working, and energetic. Tim was a law student, bursting with enthusiasm and eager to help Alison in any way he could.

They soon came upon an unusual cart. It was unlike the ones from which street vendors sold jewelry, T-shirts, or pretzels. This vendor was selling poetry.

The moment Alison laid eyes on the man behind the cart she did a double take, and her heart did a little back flip. It was Walter Williamson, an old college classmate. Back in college Alison had admired Walter's poetry and, to tell the truth, had had a crush on him as well. He had a sleek theatrical appearance about him, and his ponytail added to his writer's image. He was a proud man with a good heart, but he sometimes took himself too seriously.

"Oh my gosh!" Alison gasped. "Walter? Walter Williamson? Is it really you? I can't believe it. I mean, it's been years since I last saw you. Walter Williamson. My gosh . . . oh, I'm forgetting my manners. Tim, this is . . ."

"Walter Williamson?" Tim guessed.

Alison just babbled on. "Yes. Walter is a great writer. A wonderful poet." Then she began to get a little sentimental. She turned to Walter and said, "Oh, I still remember the poem you gave to me at graduation. Just a beautiful, beautiful poem. How did it go? Something like . . .

Good-bye, warm sun, as you sink
in the ocean,
Farewell, sweet sun, as your rays fade . . .

uh . . . something, something. I can't remember the whole thing, but it was a beautiful poem. Sad, but beautiful. Very beautiful and very moving. But . . ."

"Sad?" Tim asked.

"Yes," Alison replied, "very, very sad. How do you do that, Walter? How do you write something so emotionally complex in just a matter of a few lines? I could never express that type of emotion through writing. I've tried. But it's very tough. You were always so good with the, you know, those adverbs and nouns and . . ."

"You mean the words?" Tim prompted.

"That's it," said Alison, "the words. Of course, the words. Who could forget the words? Especially the ones that rhyme. Wow! Those are really something."

Alison fell silent, and there was a lull in the conversation. Suddenly Walter spoke up. "Who are you?" he asked.

"Oh, I'm sorry," Alison answered. "You don't remember me? Alison Krempel, from college. Don't you remember that night at the sock hop?"

"Oh, right, right. Alison Krempel," said Walter. "Wow, it's been such a long time. Well, thank you for all those wonderful compliments."

"Oh, you're welcome," said Alison. "I always loved your work. And look at this, you're selling your poems now. That's just great."

"Not really," Walter replied.

"No? But why not? What's the matter?" Alison asked.

Walter explained that he had started his business a few months before. He hadn't been very successful until he came up with a great idea—writing poems for people whose pets had died. Sometimes he even wrote poems to memorialize people's dead plants. He especially liked writing about plants because flowers made such beautiful poetic images. He pointed to a sign tacked on the front of his cart. It said:

If something has died that
  once made you happy,
Bring back the memories with a
  poem that's real snappy.
And here's my guarantee: Pets,
  plants, or whatever,
If it's dead I'll memorialize it
  with a beautiful poem you'll
  cherish forever.

(Satisfaction guaranteed or
  triple your money back.)

"Why a triple-money-back guarantee?" Alison asked.

"I needed a sales pitch," Walter told her. "It worked for a tire company that was advertising on TV. So I figured, why not me?"

"I must say, Walter, this sounds like a great idea," Alison declared enthusiastically.

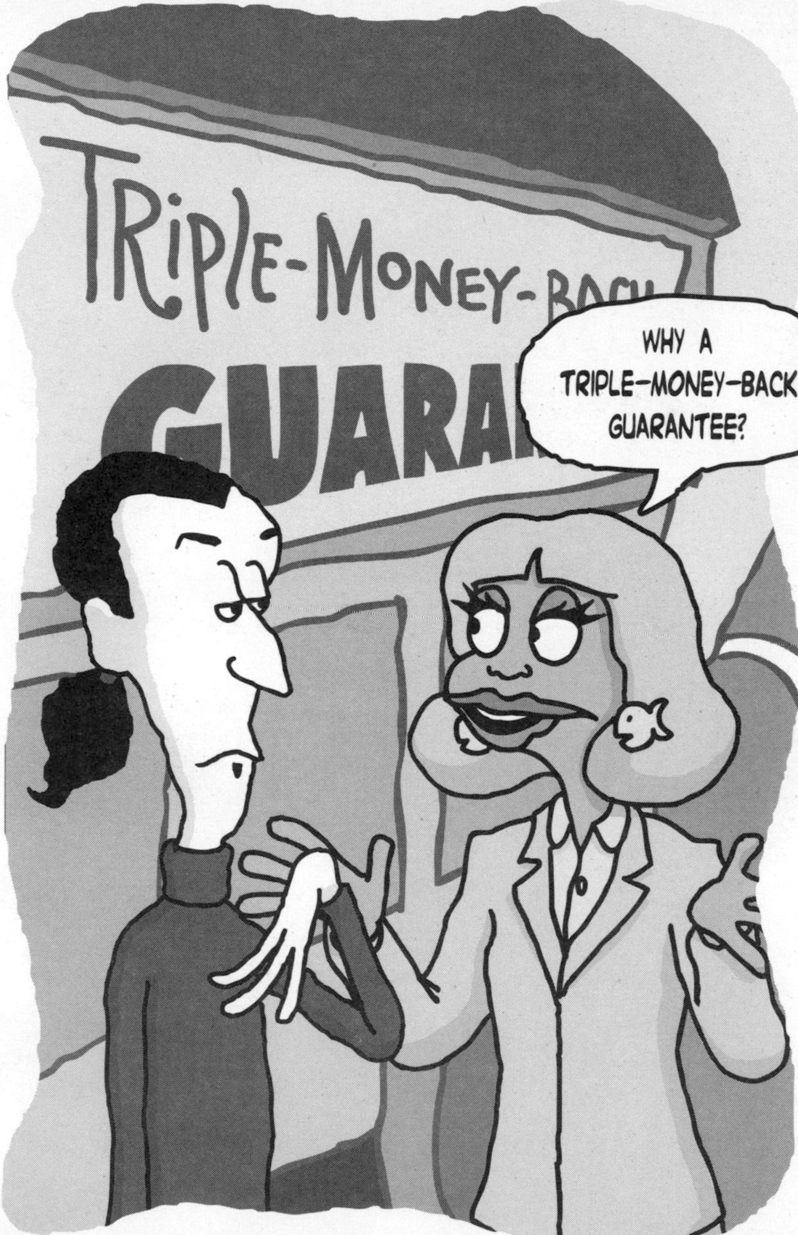
TRIPLE-MONEY-BACK
GUARAN
WHY A TRIPLE-MONEY-BACK GUARANTEE?

2

A POET WITH A PROBLEM

Just then Stenographer Fred came skipping down the street. Fred was the official Science Court stenographer. It was an important job, recording everything

A STENOGRAPHER WRITES DOWN EVERYTHING PEOPLE SAY IN COURT, USING A SPECIAL WRITING SYSTEM, AND LATER TRANSCRIBES IT.

everyone said in court, and Fred wanted to be the best stenographer he could possibly be. That's why he liked to skip sometimes. He said it was good exercise, and a stenographer always needed to be in top shape.

"Hi, Alison. Hi, Tim," said Fred, only slightly out of breath.

"Hello, Stenographer Fred. How are you?" Alison replied.

Tim and Fred greeted each other with the stenographer's handshake, wiggling their fingers together as if they were typing.

Fred turned to Walter and said, "I need a poem written for my hamster."

"Is he dead?" Walter asked.

"Oh gee, I hope so," said Fred. "I just buried him."

"Oh, I'm sure he was," Walter replied reassuringly. "What was his name?"

"Gunter," said Fred. "And could you say

something about the wheel? He loved the wheel."

"Of course," said Walter. "You know, I understand that the loss of a pet is difficult."

"He's not lost," said Fred. "He's dead."

Walter changed the subject and told Fred that the cost for one poem was only five dollars—twenty dollars including the frame.

"Just the poem," said Fred.

"Okay." Walter nodded. "Well, how about something like . . .

Gunter, you've gone, like the summer
in September.
But your cute little squeal and your
zest for the wheel
Are things that I'll always remember."

"You got anything else?" Fred asked.

"I'll work on it," Walter promised. "Come back in an hour."

"Okay," Fred agreed. "But I might be back sooner. I don't have a watch. Bye." And off he went, skipping down the street.

"So anyway, Walter," Alison said, getting back to the subject, "what's the problem?"

Walter went on to explain how, a couple of weeks before, a woman had offered to pay him a thousand dollars in exchange for writing poems for her for a whole month.

"Wow!" Tim chimed in. "That's a lot of dead pets."

"That's just what I said, 'Wow!'" Walter responded. "So I did it. At first it was the usual. I wrote a poem about her pet turtle that died and one about her parakeet that died."

Suddenly Fred reappeared. "Has it been an hour?" he asked.

"No," Walter answered.

"Okay," said Fred. And just as suddenly he was gone again.

Walter continued with his story. "But then it started getting weird. She asked me to write a poem about a wallet. She said it had been in her family for years. But I said no. And then she wanted me to write a poem about some brine shrimp eggs and a chicken bone."

"What?" Alison cried in disbelief.

"What's a brine shrimp?" Tim asked.

"Just a small shrimp," Walter explained. "She had some of the eggs."

"And why a chicken bone?" Alison asked.

"She said it held sentimental value," Walter told her. "I said I'm sure it does—for the chicken—but I still refused. I have my principles, after all. I'm a serious poet."

With her shrewd legal mind, Alison instantly guessed that Walter was being set up for a lawsuit.

"She's taking me to Science Court," Walter moaned. "That's where science is the law and scientific thinking rules."

"We're familiar with it, Walter," Alison

said. "Actually, I'm a Science Court attorney, and Tim is my assistant."

"No kidding?" Walter replied. "That's great. I mean, that's wonderful. Can you help me?"

"Well, I'm not sure." Alison hesitated. "What's this woman's name?"

"Clara Swindell," said Walter. "She seems to think she can prove that the chicken bone and the leather wallet are just as dead as the turtle and the parakeet, and therefore I should write poems about them or give her triple her money back."

"Wouldn't it be easier just to write the poems?" Tim asked.

"Not really, Tim," Walter replied. "I don't think she actually wants the poems. I think she believes she found a loophole in my guarantee and expects to make some easy money. Besides, it's a matter of principle. I put a lot into my work, and knowing she's taking advantage of me, well, I just can't do it. Even if it ends up costing me my business."

"So, Walter," Alison broke in, "have you been served?"

"I haven't ordered any food yet," Walter said.

"She means," Tim explained, "have you received any papers ordering you to appear in court?"

"Oh. Well, yes, I have," Walter replied. "Clara's lawyer came by the other day. Odd fellow. Fish tie. Wild hair. Looked like it might be a wig."

Alison and Tim knew right away who Walter was talking about—Doug Savage, Science Court prosecuting attorney. They'd fought many legal battles against him and knew him to be a determined, if somewhat scatterbrained, adversary.

"I offered to give most of the money back," Walter went on. "I don't have it all.

But he said no. He said Ms. Swindell wanted triple the money—three thousand dollars."

"Because of your guarantee," Alison said.

"Yeah," Walter replied. "He said I would rue the day I wrote that guarantee."

Tim remarked, "I didn't think Doug even knew what the word 'rue' meant."

"Well," said Walter, "he *was* reading it from a dictionary."

Alison summed up the situation. "So, Clara Swindell wants you to pay her three thousand dollars?"

"Yeah, but that's not all," Walter said. "She also wants to take away my license."

"Your driver's license?" Tim asked.

"No," said Walter. "My poetic license."

He pulled out his tattered, mostly empty billfold and withdrew a shiny plastic card. It was his license to practice poetry. He'd just had it renewed, and he liked the picture. He held it out for them to see. In large, bold print it said:

LICENSE TO WAX POETIC

"So," Walter pleaded, "do you think you can help me?"

"Walter, we'll be glad to help you," Alison assured him.

"That's great, Alison. Thanks!" Walter exclaimed with relief. "Boy, I'm glad you're a Science Court attorney. But weren't you going to pursue ballet?"

"You mean, you were going to be a ballerina?" Tim asked.

"Well, yes," Alison admitted. "But my first love was always science, and my second love was the law."

"And your third love was to be a ballerina?" Tim guessed.

"Well, no, actually my third love was chocolate."

"So your fourth love?" Tim continued.

"Pizza."

"Fifth love?" Tim pressed on.

"Never mind, Tim," said Alison.

Then Walter took Alison's hand and said, "Alison:

> *This sorry day has been*
> *painted bright*
> *By the muse of a gentle angel,*
> *Of lofty air and indigo hair*
> *And a smile so rare and . . . painful.*"

Tim and Alison just stared at Walter.

"Sorry," Walter said. "They're not all gems. But some rhyme."

FRED'S NEW PET

On the day of the trial, Stenographer Fred was sitting on the courthouse steps cuddling a stuffed polar bear when Science Court beat reporter Jen Betters came along. Jen was pert and perky, just like a serious TV journalist should be. She bounded up the steps and took a seat next to Fred.

"Hi, Fred. What's that?" she asked.

"It's my new pet," Fred replied. "Polly the Polar Bear."

"What happened to Gunter, your hamster?" Jen asked.

"He died," Fred explained.

"Oh, I'm sorry," Jen said sincerely.

"Well," Fred sighed, "he had a great life and was a lot of fun, but right now I just feel like having a pretend pet."

"Pretend pets are okay," Jen said.

"You know," Fred commented, "Polly is easier to take care of than Gunter, but not as much fun."

"Fred," Jen said gently, "it's okay to feel sad and miss Gunter."

"Really?" Fred asked.

"Of course it is," Jen replied. "Everyone experiences sadness. It's all a part of the glorious tapestry of life."

"But Gunter was so great," Fred moaned.

"Exactly," said Jen. "If he wasn't so great and if you didn't love him so much, you wouldn't feel sad. That's why it's okay to feel sad."

"Maybe I shouldn't have loved him so much," Fred said.

"But then he wouldn't have made you so happy," Jen pointed out.

"Maybe you're right," Fred agreed.

"Besides, Gunter would have felt sad if you didn't love him," Jen added.

"Actually," said Fred, suddenly turning practical, "a hamster can't feel human emotions, Jen. I mean, after all, it is only a glorified rodent."

"Whatever you say, Fred," replied Jen, who, besides being pert and perky, was also easygoing. "The trial starts soon. I'll see you inside." And with that she bounded the rest of the way up the steps and into the building.

DEAD OR ALIVE OR NEITHER

Inside the courtroom, Alison, Tim, and the defendant, Walter, sat at one table, while Doug and his client, the plaintiff, Clara Swindell, sat at another one just across the

WHAT'S A PLAINTIFF?

THAT WOULD BE ME, THE PERSON COMPLAINING.

aisle. Micaela was in the gallery. Micaela was a girl who loved Science Court and never missed a session. In fact, sometimes it seemed like she knew more about what was going on than anyone else did. Stenographer Fred stood in front of the courtroom, ready to address the crowd, as Jen faced the camera.

"Good morning," she began. "Welcome to Science Court. I'm Jen Betters reporting. Today is the case of poetic justice. Oh, court's about to start. Let's watch."

"All rise for the honorable Judge Stone," Stenographer Fred announced. "And all bow your heads in a moment of silence for the passing of a dear companion and all-around good hamster, Gunter."

All the people in the courtroom bowed their heads and observed a moment of silence. Meanwhile, Fred was already back in his seat, ready to begin. "How long is a moment?" he asked Judge Stone. "I don't have a watch."

"I think that's good, Stenographer Fred," the judge replied. Judge Stone ruled over Science Court. She was firm yet fair, and well accustomed to Stenographer Fred's problems with concentration.

"Thank you, everyone," she continued. "That was very sweet. So, today we have Clara Swindell suing Walter Williamson for three thousand dollars. Ms. Swindell also asks that his poetic license be revoked." Judge Stone was not familiar with the licensing requirements for poetry. She turned to Fred and asked, "Really? Can we do that?"

"Sure. Why not? You're a judge," Fred replied.

"Wow," Judge Stone exclaimed. "Okay, let's start with your opening statements. Mr. Savage . . . ?"

Dramatically, Doug Savage rose to his feet. "Thank you, Your Honor," he began. "Good morning, jury, how are you?"

"I'm a little sleepy," one of the jury members responded.

"I hate jury duty," another one said.

"I think I'm on the wrong case," yet another stated.

Doug plowed right ahead. "Good, glad to hear it. Ladies and gentlemen of the jury, definitions are great, aren't they? They tell us what things mean. And that's what this case is all about: exact scientific definitions and precise technical wording, with regard to life and death. We will prove . . . well, I will prove . . . well, one of us will prove . . . that Mr. Williamson violated his own guarantee by not writing poems about things that are . . ." Doug began to cry, ". . . dead. I'm sorry, I . . ."

The jury seemed to be deeply moved by Doug's emotional display. Until, that is, he pulled his hanky dramatically out of his breast pocket to wipe the tears from his eyes and half a raw onion fell onto the floor.

"I . . . OOPS," said Doug. "Sorry, Your Honor. That wasn't supposed to happen."

"I figured that," said the judge. "Get on with it, please."

"Okay, then," Doug continued without missing a beat. "Clara Swindell paid Walter Williamson to write some poems about things that were very dear to her, and he refused because he claimed they weren't dead. We will show that he's wrong."

Next Judge Stone asked Alison Krempel to present her opening statement.

"Thank you. Ladies and gentlemen of the jury," Alison began, "this is all very simple. We will show that the stuff is not dead and that Clara Swindell is only trying to make a quick, illegal buck."

Judge Stone then instructed Doug Savage to call his first witness, and Doug called his client, Clara Swindell, to the stand.

Clara was a thin, bony woman who always looked as if she had just stubbed her toe. As she took the witness stand, she dabbed her nose with a tissue and pretended to hold back tears.

Doug Savage approached the witness with a show of compassion. "Clara, if this is too difficult for you, let me know by sobbing loudly."

"Oooh . . . " Clara moaned as she let out a loud sob.

"Your Honor," Doug requested, "I'd like permission to continue questioning at a later time."

"Fine with me," Judge Stone agreed.

"Thank you," said Doug. "I now call Dr. Julie Bean."

Dr. Julie Bean was an expert on all things scientific. Her peculiar hairstyle made her look like an elf.

"Dr. Bean," Doug began, "will you please

explain how scientists talk about living things and other things?"

"Sure," Julie replied. "All things in our world are in one of three categories: living, non-living, or dead."

Fred chimed in, "I'm in the stenographer category."

"Actually," Julie corrected, "you're in the living category."

"Oh," said Fred.

When Doug asked Dr. Bean to give some examples of the three categories, she produced a chart and explained that a mosquito is a living thing because it can grow and reproduce, while a piece of iron is a non-living thing because it does not grow and cannot reproduce.

Fred interrupted. "By reproduce, do you mean make copies?"

"No," Julie said. "I mean make babies."

"Oh," said Fred.

Dr. Bean went on to explain that the things we call dead are things that used to be alive but no longer are.

"So," Doug pressed, "something that is dead had to be alive at one point?"

"Oh, yes, of course," said Julie. "Nothing can be dead unless it was alive first."

Doug pulled out a chicken bone and said, "Now, in which category would you put a . . . chicken bone?"

There was a strong reaction from the jury, and Clara Swindell moaned loudly as if in grief.

"I object, Your Honor," Alison broke in. "This is ridiculous."

"Give up?" Doug asked.

"No, I don't give up," Alison replied defiantly. "You should give up."

"Why should I give up?" Doug scoffed. "I'm winning."

Judge Stone banged her gavel. "Okay, that's enough. Now we're going to take a break, and I want you two to think about what you're doing. Court is recessed."

Jen Betters turned to the camera and spoke into her microphone. "Wow! Which category does a chicken bone belong to? We'll find out soon enough."

POETIC JUSTICE

With everyone back in the courtroom after the recess, Stenographer Fred stood up and announced, "Eyes up front, Judge Stone is back."

"Thank you, Fred," Judge Stone said pleasantly. "Now, we were discussing a chicken bone."

Doug nudged his client, Clara, who let out another big moan. "Your Honor," Doug said, "may we have another break? My client is having a difficult time because that dead bone meant a lot to her."

Stenographer Fred shrugged. "All rise," he began.

"No, Stenographer Fred," Judge Stone corrected. "We just had a break. Sit down, Mr. Savage."

"Your Honor," Alison interrupted, "Mr. Savage is calling this chicken bone 'dead.' But it is not dead, because it was never alive to begin with."

The jury mumbled. Could a chicken bone be dead if it had never been alive in the first place? They didn't know, but they wanted to find out.

With Judge Stone's permission, Doug Savage went on with his questioning. "Now, Dr. Bean, you're a learned person, are you not?"

Julie Bean did not know quite how to respond to that. "Ah . . . Uh . . ." was all she could say.

"Is this bone alive?" Doug asked her.

"Nope," Julie replied.

"Is it . . . non-living?" Doug asked.

"Nope," said Julie. "It's not non-living either."

At this the jury went wild.

"So then there's only one category left," Doug said.

"Is it a stenographer?" Fred asked.

"No, Stenographer Fred, it isn't," Doug replied. "But it isn't living and it isn't non-living, so it must be . . . dead."

Again the jury went wild.

"But how can that be?" Alison asked, genuinely puzzled. "That chicken bone couldn't live on its own."

"Only organisms—independent living things—can do that," Julie explained. "But parts of organisms can also be living."

"Look at me," Doug said, beaming with pride. "I'm absolutely beaming with pride."

"Think about a leaf on a tree," said Julie.

"The tree is a living organism, but the leaf is also alive. It's made of cells that grow and reproduce. But if the leaf is separated from the tree, like the chicken bone from the chicken, it dies."

Clara Swindell let out a loud moan and pretended to faint into Doug's arms.

"You're a little heavy for this, Clara," Doug whispered, as he struggled to hold her upright.

Stenographer Fred was puzzled. "How can a leaf be made out of jail cells?" he asked.

"Not that kind of cell, Fred," Judge Stone answered. "A cell is the smallest part of a living thing. In fact, some organisms are only one cell big!"

"So, Julie," Doug said, "when my client asked for a poem written for a dead chicken bone, that's scientifically accurate, correct?"

"Yes, that's accurate," Julie agreed. "It's pretty weird, but accurate."

"Thank you, Julie," Doug concluded. "No more questions."

Judge Stone turned to Alison. "Ms. Krempel, any questions?"

"No questions," Alison replied.

Doug thought he'd proved his point, so he rested his case. Then it was Alison Krempel's turn.

"Ms. Krempel," Judge Stone said, "you may call your first witness."

At first, Alison didn't realize that Judge Stone was speaking to her, since she and Tim were reading a book entitled *The Amazing Brine Shrimp*. On the book's cover was an illustration of a shrimp wearing a superhero costume with a cape.

"Uh . . . Ms. Krempel?" Judge Stone repeated, trying to get Alison's attention.

"Oh, sorry, Your Honor," Alison said, quickly rising to her feet. "I call Professor Parsons to the stand."

Professor Parsons was another Science Court science expert. He was particularly expert, in fact, on the subject of brine shrimp, which was appropriate since he was sort of a shrimp himself.

"Now, Professor Parsons," Alison began, "could you please tell the court what . . . these are?" With a flourish she produced some brine shrimp eggs.

The jury's reaction was powerful.

"Those are brine shrimp eggs," Professor Parsons said. "I should know, I'm an expert."

THEY DON'T LOOK LIKE MUCH NOW, BUT JUST WAIT!

"Are the eggs breathing or moving?" Alison asked.

"Oh, no," Professor Parsons declared. "Nada. Nothing."

"Oh, my poor brine shrimp eggs," Clara Swindell burst out. She stood up so she could faint into Doug's arms again. But he forgot to catch her, and she crashed to the ground.

"Sorry," Doug whispered as he hoisted her to her feet.

Alison went on with her questioning. "Are the brine shrimp eggs growing or reproducing?"

"Nope," said Professor Parsons.

"Oh, those poor brine shrimp eggs," Doug exclaimed. "Ohhh . . . the humanity." And with that he fainted into Clara's arms. But she wasn't strong enough to hold him, and they both toppled over.

"Mr. Savage," Judge Stone admonished. "Will you please refrain from feigning fainting?"

"What?" Doug asked.

"In other words, knock it off," said Judge Stone.

"Yes, ma'am," Doug answered humbly.

"So, Professor," Alison continued, "these eggs show no scientific signs of being alive, is that correct?"

"Correct-a-mundo," replied the happy professor.

"But the brine shrimp egg is a pretty amazing little creature, is it not?" asked Alison.

"Oh, yes, it certainly is," Professor Parsons responded enthusiastically. "Given a little time and the right conditions, I could show you some pretty amazing things, let me tell you." As if from nowhere, Professor Parsons produced a tank of salt water. "If we put our little egg friends in salt water at a temperature of 21° centigrade . . ."

"They'll freeze," Doug interrupted.

Professor Parsons reminded Doug that 21° centigrade, or Celsius, was the same as 70° Fahrenheit.

Doug pulled a thermometer out of his pocket. "Wow, he's right. That's a nice temperature for swimming."

"Of course I'm right," said the professor. "It's my job. So, now we add some fish food, and we will see that these eggs could not be considered to be dead."

"What?" Doug asked. "Fish food?"

"Fish food," the professor confirmed.

"This is fascinating," said Alison.

"Oh, I'll say," Professor Parsons agreed. "You've got to love science, don't you? But this could take about, oh, I'd say two days."

Alison addressed the bench, requesting that everyone in the courtroom be ordered to

stay for two days until Professor Parsons was finished with his experiment.

"I object," Doug objected. "I can't just sleep over. I don't have my toothbrush or my teddy bear or my teddy bear's toothbrush."

"Is this really necessary, Ms. Krempel?" Judge Stone asked.

"Very necessary, Your Honor," Alison replied. "After all, it's in the name of poetic justice, and in the name of science."

"In the name of science," Professor Parsons agreed.

"Okay," said Judge Stone, banging her gavel. "In the name of poetic justice and in the name of science, set up camp. We're staying."

COURTHOUSE CAMPOUT

At Judge Stone's instruction, the courtroom was transformed into a campsite with tents for all and everything else that makes a camp a camp. Before long, everyone was gathered around a campfire in the middle of the courtroom. Micaela was softly playing her harmonica while Walter told ghost stories. Because Walter was a poet, even his ghost stories rhymed:

> *"It was a stormy night at the old*
> *courthouse many years ago.*
> *The wind was howling a terrible*
> *howl that scared the people so.*

They heard the banging of the shutters
  outside, while inside they shivered in
  fright.
Then they heard a cry outside the door
  that turned their faces white.
Suddenly the door creaked open, slow
  at first, then fast.
The people closed their eyes so tight,
  wishing the moment would pass.
Then it was quiet, and that
  was strange.
But alas, what was even stranger
  was that
When they opened their eyes they saw
  it was only Gavel, the courthouse cat."

Everyone in the room was frightened by the story. Stenographer Fred, in particular, was shivering with fear, while Doug was hiding behind Clara Swindell as if an evil cat might leap on him at any moment.

"Great story, Walter," Judge Stone said. "Okay, lights out."

Nobody wanted to go to sleep yet, so Judge Stone agreed that, just this once, they could stay up as long as they liked. And they did, telling stories and singing campfire songs until almost eleven o'clock.

THE BRINE SHRIMP MIRACLE

Two days later the campout was over. The courtroom was returned to normal, except that there was a charred spot on the floor where the campfire had been. Everyone was in his or her place when Stenographer Fred announced, "All rise and all shine. That includes you, Judge Stone." He lifted a pink, frilly blanket, but Judge Stone was not there. She was already seated at the bench.

"Uh, Fred," she called, "I'm up here."

"Oh," said Fred.

Just then Doug stuck his sleepy head out

from under a blanket and patted Fred on the shoulder. "Umm, just five more minutes," he mumbled groggily.

But Judge Stone banged her gavel with authority and called, "Okay, order. Order. Ms. Krempel, how's the professor's experiment going?"

"Good, Your Honor," Alison replied. She turned to Professor Parsons, who was already seated on the witness stand. "Isn't that right, Professor?"

Professor Parsons pointed to the tank full of new baby brine shrimp. "Absolutely," he replied. "As you can all see, the eggs have produced baby brine shrimp."

The jury applauded to express its amazement.

"Wow."

"That's amazing."

"Incredible."

"I want to go home."

"So the eggs were alive after all," Alison continued. "Well, my client certainly could not have written a poem memorializing something that was still alive."

"Wait a minute. Objection," Doug objected. "Your Honor, just two days ago, Professor Parsons said the eggs had no signs of being alive."

"This *is* a little confusing, Professor," Judge Stone remarked.

"Oh, I know," Professor Parsons replied. "Let me try and clear some things up. Scientists have decided that even if a thing does not behave at all like a living thing, it is alive as long as it has potential. That's the key word—potential. Can you say potential?"

"Po-ten-tial," said Fred.

"Po-ten-tial," said Doug.

"Very good." Professor Parsons smiled.

"But what exactly does it mean?" Doug asked.

Professor Parsons explained that the word "potential" has several meanings, but in this case it describes something that has the capacity or ability, in the future, to produce organisms that can grow and reproduce. Therefore, he went on, something with potential is technically and scientifically considered to be alive.

"Your Honor, we rest our case," Alison declared triumphantly.

"Wait!" Doug cried out. "I want to call Professor Parsons to the stand."

"You don't have to call him to the stand. He's still there," Judge Stone pointed out.

"Hello." The professor smiled again.

"Oh yeah," said Doug. "I forgot. Now, Professor, the chicken bone was dead, right?"

"Right," said Professor Parsons.

"But the brine shrimp eggs were alive, right?" Doug asked.

"Right," the professor agreed.

"So," said Doug, "that's one for the good guys and one for the bad guys."

"Objection," Alison objected.

"Okay, okay. One for the bad guys and one for the good guys."

"Better," said Alison.

"Anyway," Doug continued, "there's still a third and final thing Walter refused to write a poem for. And this, dear people, I call my 'coop de something.'"

"Do you mean your *coup de grace?*" Judge Stone asked.

"I have no idea," Doug replied.

"Never mind," Judge Stone sighed. "Go ahead."

"I offer this," Doug said dramatically. "A leather wallet!"

COUP DE GRACE?

IT'S FRENCH FOR "STROKE OF MERCY." IT MEANS THE WINNING MOVE, YOU KNOW.

IT'S ALIVE! MAYBE

The jury murmured with interest as Doug handed them the wallet for inspection.

"This is interesting."

"A wallet."

"Nice leather."

"Is it full of money?"

"Go ahead," said Doug. "Look at it. Touch it. It's real leather. Besides carrying a lot of money for Clara Swindell, this wallet also carries a lot of sentimental value. This leather once belonged to a very dear cow." Doug sniffled as if holding back tears.

"I'm not going to faint anymore," Clara declared. "My fanny's sore."

"Now, Professor," Doug went on, "the chicken bone is alive while it's part of a living chicken, isn't that right?"

"Yep, that's right," said Professor Parsons.

"And then later, when it's not part of the chicken," Doug continued, "it's considered dead, right?"

"It can also be considered good eatin'," Professor Parsons joked. "But yes, that's right."

"So," said Doug, "was the skin of a cow ever alive when it was part of the cow?"

Alison turned to Tim. "Uh-oh," she whispered.

Tim had a sinking feeling about this.

"Well . . . ?" Doug pressed.

"Okay . . ." said Professor Parsons. "You're waiting with baited breath, aren't you?"

"My breath smells like worms?" Doug asked.

"Well, actually, yeah, it does," said Professor Parsons. "But that's not what I meant."

"So, Professor," said Doug, "is the skin of a cow alive when it is part of the cow, or is it not?"

"Absolutely," the professor replied. "Just like the leaves on a tree. It's as alive as the nose on my face."

The members of the jury murmured among themselves. They knew the trial had reached a critical point. If the wallet was no longer alive, then it must be dead, and Walter Williamson should have written a poem about it.

Walter turned to Alison and asked, "Is he saying the wallet's dead?"

"I hope not," Alison replied.

Professor Parsons produced a chart

showing parts of a skin cell. He explained that the cells of a cow's skin, just like the cells of a person's skin, are a part of a living, growing organism. "Skin is an incredible thing," he said. "In fact, why don't you give me some right now?" He put out his hand for Doug to rub.

"You want some of my skin?" Doug asked.

"I want you to skin me, man, you dig? Like, slip me some skin, Daddy-o," the professor replied. "Geez, these kids today, huh? Whataya gonna do?"

Doug halfheartedly slid the palm of his hand across that of Professor Parson's. "Anyway," Doug went on, "when the skin is no longer part of the animal—because it has been made into leather—we would have to call the skin, or the wallet in this case, dead. Isn't that right, Professor Parsons?"

"Boy, you really, really want me to say

yes, don't you?" Professor Parsons teased.

Doug nodded like a dog with a big toothy grin.

"If the wallet is considered dead," the professor went on, "then you win two out of three and probably win the case, right?"

Doug nodded again.

"That would be your first, I believe, wouldn't it?" the professor asked.

Doug nodded so hard it seemed as if his head might fall off.

"Uh, Professor," Judge Stone broke in, "as much as we're all enjoying this, I must ask you to answer the question. Is the wallet considered dead?"

"Oh, all right," said Professor Parsons. "The answer is dead, no, alive, no . . . wait."

"Professor, please," Judge Stone urged.

"Oh, okay," the professor went on. "The answer is, no, the wallet is not dead."

There was an uproar in the jury box.

Not dead. Not alive. What next?

"Whew." Alison breathed a sigh of relief.

Fred was frightened. "It's alive!" he cried. "Quick! Show it your credit cards! It's afraid of them!" He began waving a credit card at the wallet.

Micaela piped up from her seat in the gallery. "Fred, the wallet's not alive."

"Wait a minute," said Doug. "What's going on?"

"You see, Mr. Savage," Professor Parsons explained, "there's one more technicality here. If a living part of a living thing is put through a process—that's a very important word—process. Can you say process?"

"Pro-cess," said Fred.

"I can say it, but I'm not going to," Doug declared stubbornly.

Professor Parsons went on to explain that if something is put through a process to make it into something else, then the new thing that results becomes a product. Scientifically speaking, a processed product is considered non-living just like other non-living things that were never alive to begin with—a television, for instance, or a pocket protector, or a plastic milk jug.

"But how can this be? I was going to win," cried Doug.

"It's not just wallets," Professor Parsons added. "Lemonade is made from lemons, and it's considered non-living."

"Like paper from trees?" Micaela asked.

"Yes, that's right," Professor Parsons answered. "Paper comes from trees, but it must go through a process first, before it becomes paper for us to write on. So, that paper is non-living."

"But that's just a technicality," Doug objected. "The leather came from the cow, therefore it should be considered dead. D-E-D. Dead."

"Sorry," said Professor Parsons, "but the scientific definition says it's been processed, so it's non-living. Your logic is almost as bad as your spelling."

Doug was pouting now. "Well," he said, "the Savage definition says . . ." and he made a disgusting raspberry noise with his lips.

"Real mature," said Micaela.

"Stenographer Fred," Alison said, "since Mr. Savage is regressing anyway, why don't we look back at his opening statement."

"Okay," said Fred. Reading from the transcript, he began, " 'Thank you, Your Honor.' "

"No, no, after that," said Alison. "What did he say this trial was about?"

"Oh," Fred mumbled. "He said—I got it right here—he said, 'This case is all about exact scientific definitions and precise technical wording.' "

Doug made another, even louder raspberry noise.

"Mr. Savage, please stop that," Judge Stone scolded. "You're spraying everyone."

"I'm sorry, Your Honor," Doug said. "But . . ."

"I know you're only expressing your disappointment. Everyone has the right to express his or her feelings, but that's no way to do it," said Judge Stone. "Now, pull yourself together and let's hear your closing argument."

"Oh, all right," Doug huffed. Then he cleared his throat, straightened his tie, and approached the jury box with all the dignity he could muster. "Ladies and gentlemen of the jury, Walter Williamson did not live up to his part of the deal with my client to write sad, sweet poems memorializing her dead things."

As Doug spoke, Clara moaned loudly with fake grief.

"We proved," Doug continued, "beyond a shadow of a doubt, that the chicken bone is dead."

"Ooh," Clara moaned.

"Look at Clara," said Doug. "She's sad. She's grieving. She needs chicken-bone closure in her life in order to move on. And she can move on better with an extra three grand in her wallet."

"Oooh," moaned Clara.

"I want you to look into your hearts, good people of the jury, and then look this woman in the eyes and tell her that her leather wallet is not dead," Doug beseeched. "Because I can't do it. And do you know what? I don't think you can do it either."

Immediately, and with one voice, the jury turned to Clara and declared, "The wallet's not dead. It's non-living."

"Okay, okay, that's one for you," Doug admitted. "Nonetheless, Walter Williamson is guilty of having no compassion for a chicken bone that didn't hurt anyone; a brine shrimp egg that only wanted to be remembered; and a wallet that simply wanted a nice pocket, maybe something with a little ball of lint, to call home. Thank you."

"Wow," said Judge Stone. "Very moving, Mr. Savage."

"Thank you," Doug repeated smugly.

"And also very . . . disturbing," said Judge Stone. "Okay, Ms. Krempel, go ahead."

"Thank you, Your Honor," Alison said. "Ladies and gentlemen of the jury, my client is a wonderful poet. I'm sure if he wanted to, he could write a poem about absolutely anything. This pen . . ."

Walter solemnly intoned:

"The pen doth bleed its ink of blue,
Upon my fingers when snapped in two."

"Or Judge Stone's gavel," Alison went on. Walter said:

"Gavel, gavel, pounding loud,
Gavel, gavel, controls the crowd.
Forever on your memory lingers,
Because, old gavel, you smashed
    my fingers."

"You see," Alison said, "it's not a question of could he do it . . ."

Walter recited:

"Could he write those poems so sad,
Could he make one woman glad . . ."

IT'S ALL SO SIMPLE. LIVING THINGS ARE THINGS THAT MOVE AND GROW. DEAD THINGS ARE THINGS THAT USED TO BE ALIVE, OR PARTS OF LIVING THINGS. NON-LIVING THINGS GO THROUGH A PROCESS TO BECOME A PRODUCT.

"Okay, Walter, that's enough now," said Alison.

But Walter wouldn't stop:

"No more was needed,
It had all been said . . ."

Sternly, Alison said, "Quit it." Then she continued her closing argument. She told the jury that Clara Swindell had tried to make an easy buck. Clara thought she had found a loophole in what is considered to be dead. But science already has its own definitions of what is living, non-living, and dead.

As Alison finished her closing argument, Doug sat sullenly staring at the wallet on the table before him. "I think it moved," he said to Clara.

"It's not going to open up for you, if that's what you're getting at," Clara replied crankily.

"Okay, jury," Judge Stone declared, "this case is all yours. Go deliberate to your heart's content." She banged her gavel and called a recess to give the jury time to reach a verdict.

9

THE TALKING BRIEFCASE

Stenographer Fred spent the recess time trying to feed his stuffed bear spoonfuls of baby food. "Choo choo," he said. "Open up the tunnel, here comes the train." And, "Whir, whir, open up the hangar so the airplane can land." But the stuffed bear would not open its mouth, and the baby food just dribbled down its chin onto the bib Fred had tied around the bear's neck.

It wasn't long before the jury returned with their verdict and Fred had to get back to his official duties. "Don't worry, little fellow,"

he said to the bear. "We'll finish your supper later." Then, in his most official tone of voice, he announced, "Here comes the jury. Let's give them a nice round of applause."

As soon as the members of the jury had filed back into the room and taken their seats, Judge Stone said, "Okay, jury, what's your verdict?"

The jury foreperson stood up and announced, "We, the jury, find the defendant, Walter Williamson, not guilty."

"We lost," Clara said.

"Look at the bright side," Doug replied. "I won an argument."

The foreperson continued, "We feel that two out of the three items discussed were not dead, so Walter did not have to write poems for them."

"But what about the chicken bone?" Doug asked. "That was dead."

"Yes," the foreperson replied. "But we

did not think a serious poet such as Walter should have to write about a chicken bone."

"Very good, jury, very good," Judge Stone said.

"Wait," the foreperson interrupted.

"What?" asked the judge.

"We did feel, however," the foreperson went on, "that we, the jury, could write a poem about the chicken bone."

"What?" Judge Stone asked again.

"This is so sweet." Doug chuckled.

The foreperson proceeded to recite a poem:

*"Once you were a happy bone, living
   in a chicken.
Now it's like you've turned to stone
   and taken quite a lickin'.
But, chicken bone, don't you cry, you
   had yourself a treat.
You spent some time in a thigh, be
   glad you weren't in some pig's feet."*

"That's enough, that's enough," Judge Stone insisted. "Court's dismissed." She banged her gavel. "Now you can do whatever you want. You're on your own."

Doug handed Clara the chicken bone on a platter. "Here," he said. "I thought you might like to have this. I know it means a lot to you."

"Get that thing out of here," Clara replied testily.

"That's beautiful," Doug said, tears welling up in his eyes.

Jen Betters ran up to Doug, stuck her microphone in his face, and asked, "Mr. Savage, do you now understand the three categories of living, non-living, and dead?"

"Yes," Doug replied. "I know a chicken bone is dead, a brine shrimp egg is living, and a wallet is non-living."

"Wow," said Jen, "that's very good. Any other thoughts on the outcome of this fascinating trial?"

"For one thing, I was actually relieved to hear that leather is non-living," Doug said.

"Why is that?" Jen inquired.

"Well," said Doug, "now I know that my briefcase can't talk, so it must just be my imagination."

"Right. I guess that sums it up," said Jen. "Until next time, I'm Jen Betters, reporting from Science Court. Where science is the law and scientific thinking rules."

Doug Savage was still talking to his briefcase as everyone filed out of the courtroom and Stenographer Fred turned out the lights, picked up his polar bear, and said good night.

WHAT YOU NEED:

- 1 thin, uncooked chicken bone, such as a wishbone
- 1 jar with lid, large enough to hold the bone
- white vinegar

WHITE VINEGAR

1

Ask an adult to clean the uncooked bone, removing all muscles and tendons.

2

Allow the bone to dry overnight.

3

Place the bone in the jar. Add enough vinegar to cover the bone.

4

Secure the lid and allow the jar to stand undisturbed overnight.

5

Remove the bone and rinse with water.

WHAT HAPPENS:

The ends of the bone become soft first. As time passes, the bone starts to soften toward the center. The final result is a soft, rubbery bone that can be twisted.

6

Test the flexibility of the bone by bending it back and forth with your fingers. Return the bone to the jar. Repeat the flexibility test daily for seven days, letting the bone sit in the vinegar each night.

WHAT IT PROVES:

Minerals in the bone cause it to be strong and rigid. The vinegar removes these minerals from the bone, leaving it soft and pliable.

For more Science Court fun, and to find out how to bring Science Court into your classroom, visit our website.
www.TeachTSP.com/classroom/SciCourt